EROTIC ROM

Teaching SARA LOVE

Rocky Austin Quinn

WARNING

This book contains sexually explicit scenes and adult language. It may be considered offensive to some readers. This book is for sale to adults ONLY.

* * * * * * * * * * * * * * * * * * *

Please store your files wisely where they cannot be accessed by underage readers.

Please feel free to send me an email. Just know that these emails are filtered by my publisher. Good news is always welcome.

Rocky Austin Quinn - **rocky_austin_quinn@awesomeauthors.org**

About the Publisher
4Fun Publishing, a member of **BLVNP Incorporated**, 340 S. Lemon #6200, Walnut CA 91789, info@blvnp.com / legal@blvnp.com
NOTE: Due to the highly emotional reaction of some people to works of erotic fiction, any email sent to the above address that contains foul language or religious references is automatically deleted by our anti-spam software and will not be seen. All other communications are welcome.

DISCLAIMER
Please don't be stupid and kill yourself. This book is a work of FICTION. Do not try any new sexual practice that you find in this book. It is fiction and not to be confused with reality. Neither the author nor the publisher or its associates assume any responsibility for any loss, injury, death or legal consequences resulting from acting on the contents in this book. Every character in this book is over 18 years of age. The author's opinions are not to be construed as the opinions of the publisher. The material in this book is for entertainment purposes ONLY. Enjoy.

Teaching Sara Love
Erotic Romance

By: Rocky Austin Quinn

© Rocky Austin Quinn 2014
ISBN: 978-1-68030-105-2

"Jay! Phone!" I called out to my roommate Jay who was packing for a trip to Florida.

"Who is it?" He yelled back.

"Sara!"

Jay came walking into the room with a worried look on his face.

"No, it can't be this week," he said as he grabbed the phone. "Hello, Sara? Please tell me you - you are at the airport now. Damn, I could have sworn you were coming next week. I have a wedding to go to, I'll be gone all weekend. I know you can't fly back - I'm sure -," he looked at me. "I'm sure Chris won't mind hanging out with you for the week," he quietly said as he walked out of the room.

I'm sure that Sara was not thrilled about spending the weekend with me. It's not like we have issues with each other, we just have not really met before. I have probably said three words to her, all over the phone. Jay came back into the room and put the phone on the table.

"Listen man, I didn't know that Sara was coming this week. I need you to keep her entertained for the next few days. I'm the only person she knows in this state and I don't want her staying alone in a hotel room or something," Jay said as he ran back to the bedroom and grabbed his suitcase. "You can pick her up after you drop me off."

"No problem, I'm sure we could find something to do," I said while standing up and grabbing my car keys. "Let's go."

Jay grabbed me by the arm and stopped me.

"I owe you man. Just be nice to my cousin, she can be a little shy. My aunt and uncle are very strict parents and she isn't great at making friends. She won't really open up unless she trusts you," he told me in a serious tone.

"Don't worry; I'll make her feel at home," I said with a smile.

We left the apartment and headed downstairs to my old Ford Taurus. Jay loaded his suitcase in the back and climbed aboard. We headed off for what should have been a half-hour drive to Los Angeles International Airport. It was noon on a Friday so the traffic heading into the city was a mess, not that it isn't a pain all day every day.

After a delay, we arrived at the airport just shy of 1:00 in the afternoon. His flight was not until 3:00 so he still had plenty of time to get through security. I followed him around the airport until he found Sara. I had never seen her before so I had no idea what to expect. She was a pretty short girl, probably no taller than five-foot three. She was definitely cute, not drop-dead gorgeous but very cute and innocent-looking with long black hair that had two blond streaks running down the front. I could not tell how her body looked since she was wearing baggy black jeans and a loose-fitting black hoodie.

Jay and Sara hugged and talked for a few minutes before walking towards me.

"Chris, this is Sara. Sara, this is Chris," Jay said.

"Hi," she softly said, visibly shy.

I could see that her mouth was fitted with braces.

"Hi Sara," I responded.

"Well guys, I got to head off," said my roommate. "See you guys in a week."

Jay headed towards security and left me alone with his cousin.

"Come on Chris, let's get out of here," Sara said while forcing a smile before following me outside.

For the entire hour long ride home, Sara looked out the window and said nothing. Since Jay had told me that she was extremely shy, I did not try to force anything. I knew that when she wanted to talk, she would talk.

Once we made it out of the city, we finally started making good time. In no time, we were at the apartment. I got out of the car and started towards the door but Sara remained in her seat. I walked over and knocked on the window, causing her to jump. She looked up at me from inside.

"Sorry," she said.

I opened the door for her.

"No need to apologize," I told her as I grabbed her bags from the backseat and led her inside.

Sara politely opened the apartment door for me as I carried her two bags inside. I took them into Jay's room and placed them on the bed.

"You can stay in Jay's room. I don't think he will mind," I said as she entered the room

"Thank you for carrying my bags. That was really nice," she said as she fought back a smile.

"Don't worry about it. If you need anything, just ask."

I started to head out the door when she grabbed my arm.

"Sorry but where...where is the bath...the, uh...," she shyly stammered

"Bathroom is right next door," I told her with a friendly smile.

Sara followed me out of the bedroom as I pointed the bathroom out to her. She kept her eyes down as she walked in and slowly closed the door. Instead of being a creep and waiting for her to finish, I walked over to the couch and sat down. After a minute, I heard her open the door. I looked back and saw her standing outside of the door staring me. Once our eyes met, she smiled and looked at the ground before walking into Jay's room.

An hour later, I sat there watching the football game from the night before on the DVR. I tried to focus on the game but I was too busy wondering what Sara was doing in the room. Jay did not have a television or computer in his room and from what I felt carrying her bags, she didn't bring anything besides clothes. I got up from the couch and walked over to the door. I lightly knocked.

"Sara?" I called out.

"Yes Chris?" she instantly called back.

"Can I come in?" I asked.

"Yes."

"Hi, Chris," she said as I opened the door with a smile on her face.

"Hey. So what have you been doing in here?" I asked, not trying to sound creepy or invasive.

"Nothing. I've just been laying here," she said

"Aren't you bored?"

I sat down on the bed and she scooted away.

"Yeah a little," she nervously said.

"Why don't you come out to the living room and watch some TV with me?" I asked as I stood up and reached my hand out.

"I…I don't know. I don't think I'm allowed," she responded, causing her smile faded away.

"Allowed? Why would you not be allowed?" I asked, confused.

"Mom and Dad only let me watch TV on Sundays. They say that I'm not to watch TV any other day or I'll be in trouble," she said as she brought her knees to her chest.

"Wow, Jay wasn't kidding. Your parents are strict," I said, receiving and agreeing nod. "Come watch TV with me, I won't tell them. Promise."

I stood back up and again reached my hand out. Sara looked back up at me, smiled and grabbed onto my hand. I led her into the living room and took a seat next to her. As soon as she saw the paused screen she looked at me.

"Are you watching football?" She asked me.

"Yeah. It's the game from last night. We can watch something else if you want," I said, reaching for the remote.

"No no, I like football. It's one of the few things I watch," she said as she grabbed the remote and put it on the couch.

"Cool."

I pressed play and continued watching the game with Sara sitting next to me. As we watched the game, I could tell that Sara was starting to come out of her shell. Not that long ago, I thought she would be quiet and to herself all weekend but now she was really getting into the game. The clock came to straight zeros and the game was over, the Ravens had beaten the Bengals on a last second field goal which caused Sara to stand straight up and clap. It did not take long for me to figure out who her team was.

"Awesome. I love to see Baltimore win," she said, sitting back down and looking at me with a happy smile. "Thanks for letting me watch it."

"No problem Sara," I responded. "Anything you want to eat for dinner?" I asked as I saw the clock read 6:00.

"I can choose? I never get any say in what I eat," she excitedly said. "Is there a Subway around here? I had a sub from there a few months ago and loved it."

"You're in luck, there is one about a mile away," I said as I stood up.

"Cool. I'll go get my shoes. Thank you Chris," she said as she looked back at me.

A minute later, Sara came out of the room. She had put on the same pair of black sneakers she had worn earlier but had removed the black hoodie. Underneath, she had on a bright red t-shirt that fit well on her. For the first time, I was able to see what kind of body she had on her. Sara had a nice, slender body with an average sized set of breasts on her. She was overall a very cute girl. She had a big smile on her face as she walked towards the front door.

"Let's go Chris. I haven't eaten since I was still in Virginia," she eagerly said.

I got up, grabbed my keys and headed out. We got back in the car and took the short drive to Subway. I told her to order whatever she wanted, so she got a foot long meatball sub. I got the same and we quickly were headed back home. She held the bag of sandwiches close to her body, just waiting to get back and start eating.

"You can start eating now if you want," I told her.

"No no, it would be rude to eat while you can't. I can wait," she kindly responded.

Once we got back to the apartment, Sara ran the bag over to the living room and sat down. As soon as I sat next to her, she unwrapped one of the sandwiches.

"Here is yours, Chris," she said, handing me the unwrapped sub.

"Thank you Sara, that was very kind of you," I responded as I took the food from her.

She unwrapped the other sandwich and started tearing into it. I had not eaten since this morning either so I was just as hungry as she was. We finished our sandwiches at about the same time. She looked happy to have finally gotten food into her stomach. I stood up and grabbed all of the trash from the table.

"Do you want something to drink?" I asked her as I walked towards the refrigerator.

"What do you have?"

I opened up the fridge and looked inside.

"I've got water, soda and beer," I told her as she looked at me, indecisively. "Do you want to try a beer? I'm going to guess that you have never had one."

"I haven't but I'm only nineteen. Aren't I supposed to wait until I'm twenty-one?" she asked.

"Legally yes but almost everyone drinks before they are supposed to. I'm twenty-four and I've been drinking, not heavily though, since I was sixteen. Again, I won't tell your parents…hell, I don't even know your parents," I joked as I grabbed a beer out of the fridge and opened it up. "Just try it. If you don't like it, I won't make you drink another one."

Sara reluctantly took the beer from my hand and sniffed the bottle.

"It smells good," she told me while smiling and pressed the bottle to her lips.

Slowly, she lifted it up until the beer entered her mouth. Once she swallowed her first sip, she looked at me and smiled.

"This tastes pretty good."

She took another sip, a much bigger one. She let out a tiny burp after she swallowed. The dark-haired girl started giggling out of embarrassment.

"Excuse me," she said.

"I guess you like it. If you want more after that, they're right here," I said, pointing at the fridge.

"Thanks but I'm going to get a shower and go to bed after I finish this one." She said as she took another large gulp of the beer.

"I understand; you had a long day. Towels and everything you need are in the bathroom," I explained.

"Okay thanks. You have been really nice to me today Chris - thank you." she responded as she finished her beer.

"No problem. You are my roommate for the next week, I don't want to be a rude asshole," I said, making her giggle. "What?"

"You said 'ass'. I know it's not funny but I never hear words like that at home," she explained, looking nervously at me and waiting for me to laugh...which I did. "I'm gonna take a shower now."

She stopped in Jay's room to gather new clothes before walking into the bathroom. I relaxed on the couch with a beer and watched TV while Sara showered in the next room. I was feeling really tired really quickly even though it was only 8:00, I turned the TV off and started walking towards my room after tossing the bottle away. I was not paying attention and did not notice Sara coming out of the bathroom. I ended up walking in to her, almost knocking her to the ground but I grabbed her arm in time.

"I am so sorry Sara, I didn't see you," I apologized as I pulled her back up.

"It's okay. It wasn't your fault," she smiled. "Good night."

I let go of her and she went into Jay's room, waving at me before closing the door. I headed to my room and immediately passed out on the bed.

Around two o'clock, I woke up with a very full bladder needing release. In my groggy state, I walked towards the bathroom but forgot to notice the light shining from under the door. I opened the door and was met by the bright light. Quickly, I focused my eyes and saw Sara on the toilet, her pink shorts down around her ankles and her hairy pussy in full view.

"AHHH!" She screamed.

I ran out of the room and closed the door.

"I'm sorry, I'm really sorry Sara." I said as I stood outside the door. "Oh god."

I waited for several seconds until she came walking out.

"I'm sorry Chris," she said, looking at the ground. "It's my fault."

She started walking away but I grabbed her arm. She quickly spun around and we met eye to eye. I noticed a tear streaming down her red cheek.

"It's not your fault...I should have knocked. I was still groggy. Do not blame yourself, it was all on me," I said, trying to make her feel better. "Don't cry Sara."

She looked up at me and forced smiled.

"Okay Chris. I guess you're right. Good night."

I used the bathroom and went back to bed. I was not sure if Sara was really okay or just putting on a brave face. Either way, I hoped that she would be back to normal tomorrow.

I woke up around six in the morning and made sure to check to before entering the bathroom. The coast was clear and took care of my business. After I finished, I exited the bathroom in time to see Sara exit Jay's room. She looked away and walked past me, obviously still embarrassed from what happened the night before.

Instead of worrying about it, I went into the kitchen and grabbed a donut for breakfast. I made a cup of coffee and sat down at the table, turning on the TV to watch the news. A few seconds later, Sara emerged from the bathroom. She stood at the door staring at me as I drank my coffee. I caught her out of the corner of my eye trying to sneak back into the bedroom.

"Sara." I called out, causing her to stop in her tracks and look back at me. "Come here, we need to talk about what happened last night."

Sara forced a smile and slowly walked towards me. She sat down across from me and tried to look away while I thought of how to start the conversation.

"About last night," I said, causing her to look up at me with a scared look. "I can't tell you enough how sorry I am about that. I should have knocked."

Sara cleared her throat and spoke.

"I'm okay Chris, I understand that it was an accident. I was just embarrassed that you saw my -my-"

"Just say it Sara, you will feel better," I interrupted.

"Hair."

"Hair?" I asked.

"Yeah. I heard that guys are disgusted when girls have too much hair around their area," she said, crossing her legs.

"You mean that is what you were embarrassed about? Not that I saw your 'area' at all?" I asked, confused.

"Well, yeah. I can't help that I have an area but I'm not allowed to shave it and I thought it made me weird," she said in a squeaky voice as her face was starting to get less red.

"Sara, guys have different tastes. Some guys like a girl to be completely shaved but some like some hair. Hell, some guys like it to be as hairy as an animal. All that matters is what you like. If you want to shave it, you are more than welcome. You can't let your parents control your life forever Sara. How will they know if you shave or not? It's not like they pull your pants down and check, right?" I said.

"No but they will freak out if I get a razor," she said with a giggle.

"Don't you shave your legs?" I asked.

"Yes I do but I have to use my mom's electric razor and I have to do it in front of her," she explained.

"You poor, poor girl," I reached out and grabbed her hand. "You really need to get out of that house."

"I know," she laughed nervously.

"Today I have to go to work. In the bathroom, there's a pack of fresh razors. If you want to…take care of the issue…you are more than welcome." I told her as I stood up and put my coffee mug in the sink.

"You are so nice to me Chris. Thank you," she said as she grabbed my hand and loosely grip my fingers.

"No problem Sara." I lightly patted her on the shoulder. "Whatever you want to do today, you can. I'm leaving at eight and won't be back until five," I explained before handing her the TV remote. "Go relax while I take a shower."

Sara took the remote and sat on the couch. I quickly took a shower and got dressed for work. Being a cashier may not be a thrilling job but I've been at the same place for eight years now and make a decent amount of money, so I cannot complain. I came out of my room and headed for the door.

"Okay Sara, I'll see you later. Remember, whatever you want to eat or drink you are more than welcome," I reiterated.

"Okay Chris. Have a nice day at work!"

She smiled at me and watched as I walked out of the apartment.

~~***~~

After a long day and a lot of asshole customers (it was a Saturday, I should not have expected less) I came home and went to open the door. I listened and heard something I was not used to hearing. I could hear Sara laughing hysterically in the apartment. I opened the door and walked in. As I walked into the living room, I saw her lying on the couch watching a comedy movie. I looked over and saw the coffee table covered in empty beer bottles. I counted at least ten bottles standing up straight with not a drop of liquid left over. I knew she was drunk off her ass because I do not buy weak beers, I only buy the strong stuff. Ten wimpy beers would make her, at her size, very drunk anyway.

"Sara?" I asked which caused her to jump.

"Hi Chris, I'm so happy to see you again," she said, slurring her words. "Guess what I did today?"

"I can see what you did, you drank a lot of beers," I said as I picked up an empty bottle

Sara struggled to stand up and keep her balance.

"No no…well, yes…but no. I did what you said I should do and I cut my hair!" she exclaimed as she grabbed my shoulders.

I looked at her head and did not notice a haircut.

"It doesn't look like you did," I said, very confused.

"No not that hair, this hair," she laughed while pointing down at her crotch. "I didn't want to get rid of it all so I took the sci-," she hiccupped. "-scissors and trimmed it up. Wanna see?"

"No Sara, I'm good. Maybe you can show me later," I embarrassingly said, regretting the words. Had she not been drunk, I probably would not have said that.

"You know what else I did?" she asked me. Before I could answer, she interrupted. "I drank this many beers!" she yelled, holding up ten fingers. "I like beer, they make me feel funny," she laughed. "Want one?"

"I'll get one. I don't think you should have another," I said as she followed me, stumbling, as I walked to the fridge.

"Is this what being drunk is like?" she asked me.

"Yes."

"I like it," she slurringly said before she sat down at the table and stared at me. "Can I ask you something else?"

"Sure," I said, sitting down with a beer and a sandwich.

"Am I pretty?"

I almost choked on my food as she asked this.

"What?"

"I said am I pretty?" she had a large smile on her face as she asked this.

"Uh…of course you are pretty Sara. You are very pretty," I said as the heat rose in my face.

"Really? Thank you Chris," she slurred as she made it to her feet and hugged me. "I think you're pretty cute," she whispered into my ear.

I was not sure if it was the alcohol talking or if she really thought that. For now, I just chalked it up to the beer.

"I think you are a little too drunk Sara, maybe you should go to bed," I suggested.

"You think so? I do feel tired…and I have to pee really badly," she said putting her hands against her crotch.

I held her hand to keep her steady and led her to the bathroom. I waited outside the door as she did her business until I heard her call out.

"Chris? Can you help me real quick?" she yelled. I opened the door and saw her sitting on the toilet with her legs spread, showing me her trimmed hair. "Did I shave this right?" she asked me as she pointed to it.

"Yes, it's fine." I said quickly before I stepped back out.

"Thank you!" she called out. About a minute later, she came out of the bathroom stumbling. "Bed time?"

"Yes, you need to sleep the drunk off."

Sara started walking with me but could not keep her balance. I picked her up and carried her into her room. She wrapped her arm around my neck and smiled at me as I placed her on the bed. I tossed the blanket over her body after rolling her onto her side.

"Good night Sara," I said as I kissed her on the cheek.

"Good night Chris," she responded before passing out.

I left her alone and continued on with my night. I showered, watched TV and went off to bed around ten o'clock. After turning the light off, I got under the covers and drifted to sleep.

Just like the night before, I had to get up and use the bathroom around three o'clock. Luckily, there was no sign of Sara when I walked in. I did my business and got back in bed. When I pulled the covers back over me, something did not feel right. I turned the lamp on and looked over to see Sara sleeping in my bed. I jumped at first and started trying to wake her up.

"Sara," I said as I shook her shoulder. "Sara, wake up."

Sara stretched and moaned as she awoke from her drunken sleep. She looked at me and jumped like I did when I saw her.

"Chris! What are you doing in my bed!?" she yelled as she held the blanket close to her chest.

"You are in my bed," I told her.

Sara looked around and gasped.

"Oh my god, I'm so sorry. I can't remember how I got here or why my head hurts so much," she said as she grabbed her skull.

"You're hungover Sara, you had too much beer while I was at work. You probably got lost on the way back to your room," I explained.

Sara looked at me with concern.

"I was drunk? Oh god! Did I act stupid when I was drunk?" she asked.

"Well you said I was 'pretty cute' and you showed me your crotch again. Other than that, you were pretty normal," I laughed.

Sara looked horrified. "I showed you my...oh god!" she said, slamming her head down on the pillow and beginning to sob.

"It's okay Sara, you were drunk. It's not your fault," I said as I lay back down on the bed and threw my arm over her. "You just wanted to show off the hair cut you gave it," I said to try and cheer her up and failing as she continued sobbing. "Please stop crying," I said as she continued crying. "Would it make you feel better if I showed you mine?"

Sara froze and looked at me.

"What did you say?" She asked.

"Would it make you feel less embarrassed if you saw my...lower regions?" I asked her.

"Maybe. I've never seen a naked guy in person," she said, perking up.

I stood up in front of her as she sat at the edge of the bed.

"Here goes nothing." I said as I pulled my sweatpants down and exposed my hard, six-inch cock to the young woman. Her jaw dropped when she saw it.

"Oh my god! It's so big," she said as her cheeks reddened.

"Thank you." I said (it's always nice to hear a girl compliment the size of your package).

"And you have a lot of hair too," she said while still lost in amazement.

"Yes. Like I told you, you weren't weird for having a lot," I explained as she smiled at me. "Did it work? Are you less embarrassed?"

"Yes, I am! Thank you so much Chris. You have a very nice pe-di- thing!" she exclaimed, looking for the right word

I pulled my pants up and lay back down on the bed. She got up and started to walk back to her room.

"If you want to stay here, you can," I yelled out.

"Really? Okay!"

Sara ran back to my bed and lay down next to me. I pulled the covers over both of us and turned the light off.

I woke up the next morning and did my usual morning stuff. I grabbed my cup of coffee and sat down on the couch. At nine o'clock, I put the football pregame show on and watched it for a few minutes before Sara came out of the bathroom.

"Hi!" she said as she sat next to me.

"Hi. How's your head?" I asked.

"It's better. Sleeping next to you made me feel better," she said with a smile. "I couldn't get the picture of your thing out of my head."

"You really liked it didn't you?" I chuckled.

"It's the first one I've seen," she commented as she placed her hand on my arm. "Can I ask you something that I've been wondering?"

"Sure, I said."

"Is it true that a guy…when he gets really excited, shoots- you know, shoots stuff out of his- thing?" I almost spit my coffee out as she asked this.

"What?" I asked her.

"Like, when I touch myself down there I get a really good feeling and some liquid comes out that isn't pee. Do guys do that to when they touch themselves?" she curiously asked.

"Didn't you learn these things in school?"

I was surprised at how little she knew but knowing how strict her parents were, I shouldn't have been.

"My parents wouldn't let me take sex-ed. They said that I would figure it out when I got married," she nervously said.

"Okay then. To answer your question, yes. When a guy's thing, his cock, gets played with he shoots thick white semen out of it. It's the same stuff that creates babies," I explained.

"So if he shoots inside a girl's thing…"

"Let's not say thing, let's call it what it is, her pussy," I interrupted.

"Inside a girl's pussy," she giggled. "Than a baby is made?"

"Yes," I said.

"Can I see the stuff?"

Again, I almost spit my drink out all over her.

"You want to see me cum?" I asked in shock.

"Cum?" she asked.

"It's another word for semen, the stuff."

"Then yes, I want to see you cum." she happily said.

"This is getting weird," I thought to myself as I looked over at the TV, seeing the football game start. "How about this Sara, we make a bet on this game. If my Raiders win, I'll show you my cum but if the Texans win I'll show you a video of someone else doing it," I proposed

She laughed and shook my hand.

"Deal!"

Sara scooted closer to me as we watched the game. It started off good for me as the Raiders had a halftime lead of 17-3. I looked over at Sara and could sense that she was starting to get a little sad but she knew that there was still more of the game left.

"Do you want a beer?" I asked as the second half was about to start.

"Yes please," the polite girl responded.

Sara nursed the beer over the next quarter of the game. She took one last gulp as the third quarter came to an end with the Raiders winning 24-13.

"Can I have another?" she asked.

"Sure thing." I said as I got up and grabbed another one. "Just don't overdo it like yesterday."

Sara smiled and took the beer. She stood up and cheered as the Texans scored a touchdown…and another…and another. The game finally ended with Houston winning 34-24. Once the game was over, she placed her hand on my thigh and giggled.

"Are you going to do it?" she asked.

"I'm a man of my word," I said as I turned the TV off and stood up.

I unzipped my jeans and pulled my pants down, followed by my underwear and let my hard cock loose once again. Sara stared at it as I grabbed onto it and slowly started stroking.

"So you just move your hand up and down until you shoot your cum?" she asked.

"Yes," I responded as I slowly started increasing the pace of my strokes.

I tried not to make it last too long since I was a bit uncomfortable doing this but I also did not want to cum too fast and make her think that it's supposed to happen that fast.

"Can I do it?" she asked, causing me to freeze.

"What? You want to do it?" I asked, causing her to nod at me. "Um...sure go ahead."

Sara scooted forward on the couch and grabbed onto my throbbing member with her small, soft hand.

"It's so soft but it's still hard," she giggled and started stroking me faster and faster.

The feeling of this innocent girl playing with my cock made it hard to hold off cumming right away. I figured now that it was best to just get it over with.

Normally when I'm getting a hand job, the girl is experienced enough to tell right when I'm about to cum so warning her is never something I instinctively do. Unfortunately, I forgot that I was dealing with a girl who had not even seen a cock before and forgot to warn her when I was about to cum.

I reached forward and placed my hand behind her head and pulled her forward. Before she could ask me why I was doing this, my cock exploded and I launched shot after shot of my thick semen all over Sara. The first few shots landed on her mouth and chin, dripping down onto her black t-shirt. She did not move as I covered her shirt with the remainder of my cum.

"I forgot to warn you, I'm sorry," I said as she looked up at me as the last few drops ran down her hand.

"Wow, that was...awesome." she started happily giggling. "That's a lot more than I have."

I sat down next to her after she released her grip.

"So I guess you liked it," I laughed.

"Should I get a towel to clean up?" she asked.

"Do you want to taste it?" I asked her.

"Taste it? People do that?" she asked with a confused look on her cum-stained face

"Yeah. Just go ahead and lick it off of your hand," I instructed.

Sara looked at her hand and slowly drew it closer to her mouth. She let her tongue slip out and gently cleaned my goo off of herself. I saw her facial reactions when the taste hit her and was surprised to see that she seemed to like it.

"That tastes really good. Kind of slimy and salty but I like it!" she said as she scooped the hanging glob from her chin and ate that up as well. "Do all guys taste the same?"

"To my knowledge, yes." I said as she continued scooping cum off of her shirt and eating it.

"You are so cool for teaching me this stuff Chris. I really like you," she smiled at me as she finished her last bit of cum.

"My pleasure Sara."

I leaned forward and planted a small kiss on her lips. I stopped when I realized what I had done.

"You kissed me," she said.

"Yes, I did." I responded.

"You are the first guy that's ever kissed me," she said with a growing smile.

Sara leaned forward and kissed me back. She tried to pull away but I grabbed her head and pulled her close for a deeper kiss. She wrapped her arms around me as my tongue made its way down her throat. We remained locked in the kiss for about two minutes before we broke it, my tongue sliding into the crevices of her brace-covered teeth.

"That was amazing," she said.

"Yes, it was," I responded, still in a daze from the long, passionate kiss.

"Chris? Since you shot your cum for me, should I cum for you?" she innocently asked.

"Only if it's okay with you, Sara. I won't ever make you do something you are not comfortable with." I calmly said as I ran my hand across her cheek.

"Okay!"

Sara pulled her sweatpants and panties down to show me, once again, her freshly trimmed pussy. Now that I was actually looking at, I noticed just how pink and fresh her small opening looked. It looked as innocent as she did.

"Do you want to touch it?" she asked me.

"I've got a better idea." I knelt down on the ground and placed my hands on her thighs. "Close your eyes," I told her.

As soon as Sara closed her eyes, I dove in and massaged her virgin lips with my tongue. She jumped at first and squeaked. Looking down at me, she opened her mouth wide and closed her eyes again before letting out a high-pitched moan.

I made sure to give special attention to her clit while I licked at her lips. My thumb gently circled around it as it slowly bulged out. I gave it a quick lick to get some moisture on it before circling it again.

"Oh my, Chris that feels, oh god, so good!" she exclaimed as her breathing got heavier.

I finally let my tongue insert itself inside Sara's rapidly moistening pussy. I could not help but nibble lightly on one of her lips as I worked her over. She clenched onto the armrest and continued letting increasingly louder moans escape her nineteen year old body. She had touched herself before but nothing beats the feeling of mouth-to-genital contact, which she was learning now.

Sara kept her eyes closed and her face pointed towards the ceiling as I continued to be the first man ever to orally please her. Her pussy had gone from mildly moist to dripping wet and I made sure to catch every last bit in my mouth. The taste of her juices were made sweeter by knowing that only I had had ever tasted them.

"Chris, oh Chris, I'm think, I think I'm gonna, gonna, oh my god!" she screamed.

Sara pressed her back hard against the couch and screamed as her juices shot from her opening and splashed into my face. I sucked hard on her pussy while continuing to rub her clit furiously, drinking up those sweet liquids. Once her climax had passed, I made sure to clean her up before getting back on the couch. I pulled her close and gave her another deep kiss while she was still trying to regain her breath. When the kiss broke, she laughed and stared into my eyes.

"That was awesome Chris…and I taste good!" she exclaimed.

We spent the next few minutes passionately making out. I could sense that Sara was probably the happiest she had ever been in her life. With such strict parents, fun is not exactly something she could have regularly. In one day she has had her first kiss, made her first guy cum and had the same guy make her cum while tasting both. Once our kiss was finally broken, she stared into my eyes with a loving look.

"Would it be weird if I said 'I love you'?" she asked me.

Normally my answer would have been 'yes' but there was something about her and the moment that made me divert from normalcy.

"Not at all Sara. I think I love you too," I said as she gasped and smiled big. "I know it isn't normal to fall for someone after a few days, there is just something about you that I love."

"Really!? Thank you so much!"

We kissed once again. After another brief make out session, we turned the TV back on and continued watching football. Neither of us had bothered to put our pants back on and made sure to check each other out when we walked to and from the bathroom or kitchen. I grabbed us each a beer and held her close as we watched the screen.

"It sucks that your cousin is coming home tomorrow," I said. "We could have so much fun."

"We can't do anything with him here?" she asked me.

"I'm sure he will have a problem with me and his cousin screwing around after knowing each other for a few days," I said as Sara started laughing. "What's so funny?"

"Jay would totally understand. When he was twenty he asked his parents if a girl he met the night before could move in with them and said 'we're in love'. We've known each other three times as longs," she explained as she looked into my eyes lovingly. "We can tell him. Who cares how he reacts?"

"I do. He pays half of the rent," I nervously said.

"Don't worry," she said, giving me a mischievous looking grin and kissed me.

We held each other on the couch and continued to watch football until the late games concluded. It was 4:30 and the Sunday night game was still an hour away so we decided to go out and grab a bite to eat. Both of us had to completely change our clothes after the lovely messes we had made on each other. Sara spent some extra time in the bathroom washing any seminal residue from her face and hair. She came out of there wearing a t-shirt and a pair of shorts, both black. I grabbed a fresh t-shirt and a pair of jeans and led her out.

We stopped at Subway, per her request, and got exactly what we had gotten on Friday night. I drove us back quickly and we ran upstairs to make it in time for the game. The restaurant was very busy so what should have been a twenty minute stop turned into an hour long adventure.

Sara and I made it back in time for the start of the game. Having not eaten much all day, we quickly devoured our sandwiches and watched the game. Before halftime, I felt her rest her head against my shoulder and softly purr. I wrapped my arm around her and hugged her close. During halftime I tried to get up but she remained still.

I muted the TV and could hear her softly snoring against me. I kissed her on the cheek and slid out from under her. I lifted her up and slowly carried her into Jay's room, lightly placing her on the bed like I had done the night before, the only difference being she was not passed out drunk tonight. I tossed the blankets over her and left her alone to sleep.

Once the game was over around nine o'clock, I slowly shuffled over to her door and opened it. I looked in and saw her slowly moving around in bed. After I flipped the light on, she froze and looked at me.

"Hi Chris," she said softly.

"Hey sleepyhead," I chuckled as I walked in. "I'm going to take a wild guess as to what you're doing."

Sara smiled and started moving her arm again, closing her eyes in the process. I tore the blanket off of her and found her completely naked, her clothes at her side and her right hand swirling around her soaking wet pussy.

"I was right!" I yelled.

"I couldn't help myself. I had a dream about you and I having, you know," she giggled as she tried not to say the word.

"Sex? Sara, you can say sex…you can say anything."

I sat down on the bed as she continued rubbing herself.

"You and I were having sex," she giggled again. "And then I woke up feeling really good."

"You were horny," I told her. "That's what it's called when you feel that way."

"I was horny so I had to take care of myself," she said as she closed her eyes again, increasing the pacing of her rubs.

"I guess the thought of sex really got you going," I said

"It did. I really want to know what sex is like," she spoke, placing her free hand on my leg.

I grabbed her hand and pulled it away from her body. Without saying a word, I picked her up and carried her out of Jay's room and into my room. It was the first time that I was able to see her sweet little breasts. They were nearly as perfect as she was; nice and perky with little buds standing straight in the air. I bent down and gently kissed one as I made it my bed. I gently placed her down and started undressing.

"Chris, what are you doing?" she asked me.

"I'm going to ask this only to make sure." I took a deep breath. "Sara, do you want to have sex for the first time right now?"

Sara's eyes grew big as she gasped. She looked down as my jeans hit the ground and my six inch cock stood straight up. She looked back up and gave me a big smile.

"Yes Chris. Yes, I want to have sex. I want to become a woman tonight!" she exclaimed.

Right away, I walked over to the side of the bed and started stroking my cock inches from her face.

"Before we start, I want you to do to me what I did to you. Open your mouth Sara," I instructed.

Sara instantly opened up and a moved my cock into her waiting mouth. I felt her tongue press against the head and almost jumped out of my skin. Her tongue was very warm and soft as it moved around every bit of my cock. The more I inched in, the more her saliva covered.

I could see the joy and lust in her eyes as my meat filled her hungry mouth, gently suckling on it like a baby on its mother's breast. I lightly petted her hair with one hand and massaged her breasts with the other. Like I said earlier, it was the first time I had seen her upper body sans clothing and I was very impressed. It was such a shame that her parents kept her from living a life because under normal circumstances, she would be fighting off hoards of men wanting a chance to get with her. I was the lucky man to break her in…and I still had some breaking in to do.

Sara reached a hand out and pressed against my thigh while I started a humping motion into her mouth. The only sound in the lightly dimmed room was that of my cock splashing in and out of her throat. I was finally at a point that I could not wait any longer. I ejected myself from her and spun her around until her legs hung off the side of the bed. I opened the drawer next to the bed and pulled out a box of condoms.

"No," she said.

"Sara, the last thing I want to do is get you pregnant." I told her as I pulled the pack of condoms from the box.

"You can pull out before you cum, right?" she said as she reached her hand around my body and gave my ass a squeeze. "Please Chris; I want to do it the right way the first time." She hugged my lower body; her face pressing against my cock. "I love you," she whispered.

"Okay, but just this once," I conceded and put the packets back in the box and put the box away.

"Thank you," she whispered after kissing the head of my cock and lying back down. "I heard that it hurts the first time. Is that right?"

"Yes. It will hurt for a few minutes but then it will feel amazing," I said as I grabbed onto her ankles and spread her legs farther apart.

"Okay. I can take a little pain. I know you wouldn't hurt me on purpose," she happily told me.

I started by rubbing my rock hard cock against her soaking wet opening. She squirmed a bit as it brushed over her throbbing, red clit. I placed the head against her lips and slowly started inserting myself. She flinched as her virgin lips adjusted to my thick cock. Within a few seconds, the entire head was engulfed in my roommate's cousin.

"Are you ready?" I asked her.

Sara nodded her head and closed her eyes, ready for her virginity to be taken away by the man she loved. I grasped onto her hips and continued pressing in until I felt her hymen pressing against me. I pulled back a little bit and thrusted forward, ripping her virginity away from her.

"Oh my fucking god!" she screamed as the pain set in. this was the first time I had heard her swear.

I remained still as her body reacted to her first insertion. She looked at me, her mouth still wide open, and arched her back.

"How do you feel Sara?" I asked her.

"It hurts a bit," she squeaked as she closed her eyes while I gently pulled back.

"Tell me when it feels better so I can keep going." I pressed my hand against her crotch and massaged her clit once again.

"Keep going," She whispered.

"Are you sure?"

"Keep going," she said louder.

I pushed forward and started fucking her very slowly, careful not to hurt her. She still flinched and gasped with each thrust but she told me not to stop, so I kept going. I took it nice and slow until I was fully sure that she was fine. It only took a few minutes before her moans of pain turned into moans of joy. I started going faster as she stretched out across the bed.

"Still hurt?" I asked her.

"Not at all Chris. It feels awesome!" she exclaimed

I took my cue and started really fucking the girl. I once again grabbed onto her hips and started moving as fast as I possibly could, slamming my throbbing cock into her tight pussy. Her moans were getting louder and louder as I went faster and harder.

"Oh yes, it feels so go, so good." she panted.

I lifted her left leg up and over my shoulder, giving me a better angle to get deeper inside her. My balls were slapping hard against her taint with each thrust. Sara started running both of her hands up and down her body, stopping to massage her breasts.

We continued in these motions for a few minutes before I pulled out and flipped her over. I quickly re-inserted my cock into her pussy from behind. I reached my hands underneath her and grabbed a handful of tender breast in each hand. She pushed herself up to give me more room, moaning louder than the crisp sound of our skin slapping against ourselves.

My hands maneuvered around her slender body until they reached her shoulders. I grabbed onto them and slammed into her hard and slow for a few seconds.

I thrusted hard a few more times before gently lifting her off of me. She got down and lay flat on her stomach just inches from my cock. She closed her eyes and opened her mouth wide while I furiously jerked myself off. I gently pulled her head back with my free hand and pointed my cock directly at her mouth. I pumped a few more times and exploded in joy.

Thick strings of cum launched forward into her waiting mouth. She giggled when the warm cream first shot to the back of her throat. More cum launched into her, landing on her tongue, her teeth, her lips…wherever it could possibly end up. The last few shots hit her on the chin and dripped down to the carpet, forming a small puddle. Once I finished cumming, she scooted forward and took my withering cock into her mouth and licked me clean. For someone with such little sexual experience, Sara cleaned my cock like a pro. When she was done, there was not as much as a single sperm left on me.

Sara looked up and showed me her mouth full of cum before taking a deep gulp, swallowing every bit of it. She opened her mouth again to show me a clean mouth. She started to get off of the ground when she spotted the puddle of drying semen on the grey carpet. She pressed her lips to the floor and lightly sucked the leftover spunk from it. When she finished, she got to her knees and gave me a hug.

"That was amazing Chris." She whispered. "I love you."

"I love you too." I responded.

I stood up with her still hugging me and placed her on the bed. I went across the room to turn the light off before I crawled into bed with my girl. I pulled the covers over us and held her close.

"Goodnight Sara."

"Goodnight Chris." We kissed and fell asleep in each other's arms.

The next day, we woke up and heard Jay returning into the living room. Before we could respond and cover anything, he walked in and saw me in bed with his naked cousin.

"Not surprised," he said before leaving the room. "I'm going to bed, just don't wake me up!" he yelled.

Sara and I looked at each other and laughed.

"Told you he wouldn't care," she said as she gave me a kiss and snuggled back up to me.

The End

Here is a sample from another story you may enjoy:

George X. Bush

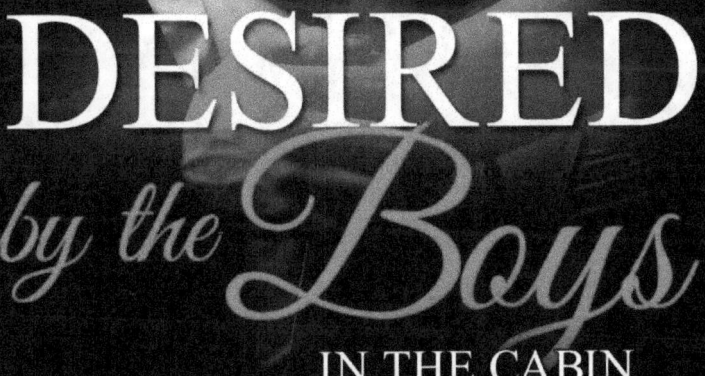

DESIRED
by the *Boys*
IN THE CABIN

Mary was fed up with being left behind each month while Riley went up to the cabin with his three friends, Mark, Robert and John, to fish, drink and just have fun. She was only 23 and she wanted some fun too, and she resented being left behind to fend for herself this way. She poured herself another drink, her third, and flopped down onto the sofa in frustration as she sipped her drink. *I'll show him*, she thought, sipping her drink, a plan coming into her head. Quickly gulping the rest of her drink down, Mary went into her room and quickly threw a change of clothes and some toiletries into a bag, grabbing her pocketbook and keys as she locked the door behind her and got into the car. If she drove steadily she could be there in three hours and surprise them.

Mary had to stop a couple of times on the way as she felt herself getting tired, but she finally pulled up to the cabin around four in the morning. As she let herself in, she heard the sounds of snoring coming from different areas of the cabin. She was tired and felt a bit ragged from all she had drunk during the evening, so she quietly tip-toed to the bathroom to take a shower. The water felt so good after the long drive and she stood under it enjoying the sensation.

When she got out of the shower and dried herself, she appraised what she was seeing in the mirror. Her long red hair hung down to the middle of her back. She had that pale skin with light freckles that was common to redheads. Her breasts were very full with large pale nipples on the ends. Mary cupped them in her hands, gently squeezing them as her fingers automatically sought out and found her nipples, squeezing them and pinching them, pulling on them as they screwed themselves into large hard knots. Her hands trailed down her flat stomach to the small thatch of bright red pubic hair that grew above her pussy. She had no hair on her pussy, having had it removed by electrolysis so that it was as smooth as a baby's. At the top of her slit her clit hood peeked through her pussy lips and her clit, fat as a pinkie finger, stuck out from beneath its hood. Her hand trailed down and her fingers trailed up through and between her pussy lips, feeling herself and the wetness that was starting. Her legs were long and straight, as were her feet and toes. Men had always found her beautiful and at the moment she quite agreed with them.

She was still squeezing her breasts with one hand, her other still between her legs when suddenly the door opened and Robert staggered in, completely naked, his cock dangling in front of him, bigger than anything Mary had even imagined. As he shut the door he blinked his eyes, trying to clear the fog of alcohol and sleep to make sense of what he was seeing.

"Mary?" he croaked, his voice still sounding a bit drunk.

"Hi, Robert," Mary said, frozen where she stood, her hands not moved.

"What're you doin' here?" he asked, slurring his words. "And how come you're naked?"

"Uh, I thought I'd drive up and surprise Riley and I just took a shower," she replied, letting her hands fall to her sides as she stared at his cock which was beginning to grow even larger.

"You sure are beautiful," Robert said, suddenly reaching out and grabbing her, pulling her close to him…

If you like this sample, look for **Desired by the Boys by George X. Bush.**

SHYLA STARR

LOVE
Anew

LONELY BILLIONAIRE ROMANCE SERIES, BOOK 1

Tricia reached for another blanket. "Are you cold?" she asked.

Rebecca's breath was raspy as she responded. As her lungs shut down due to ALS, or Amyotrophic Lateral Sclerosis, her ability to speak had started to decline. Muscle by muscle, ALS targeted the body and made it impossible for the individual to live a normal life. It had started a few years ago with Rebecca's legs. Now, her lung muscles were starting to freeze as well. Tricia winced as she thought about the future. If Rebecca chose to use machines to stay alive, her entire body would eventually stop working. At some point, her mind would remain functioning and she would be locked into her body.

Rebecca managed to squeeze out a feeble yes. Reaching over to the cupboard, Tricia removed a blanket and carefully tucked her in. Tricia had spent years training to be a nurse and really liked her job. Since she was an excellent nurse, she had caught the eye of the billionaire, John, at one of the couple's many trips to hospitals around the country. He had noticed the love and care she took with each patient. After a moment's hesitation, Tricia had allowed him to convince her to take care of his wife.

Pictures of Rebecca dotted the room. Since she was unable to leave, John had striven to make her room look like favorite memories of her life and activities. A young, healthy Rebecca smiled in each photo. In the few years she had been physically active, she had acquired awards for horseback riding, cooking and other projects. Now, though, this time of physical fitness had passed. Instead of dashing through the fields on her favorite horse, Rebecca spent her time in this room. She had taken her difficulties in stride and was truly brave in the face of all of these medical issues.

Finishing with the blanket, Rebecca started to say something. Leaning closer to hear her, Tricia finally pulled up a chair. "What do you need, Rebecca?" she queried.

Sighing, Rebecca whispered, "I need to talk to John. I have to tell him how I want to die."

Squeezing her hand, Tricia nodded. "Once I leave your room, I will go get him. Just in case he is not around, did you want me to give him a message?"

Rebecca tried to nod, but her head did not respond all the way. "Yes, I do. You need to tell him that I do not want any machines. He could keep me alive forever with a breathing tube, but I do not want to live a life where I am permanently locked into my body. And," she paused and struggled to take another breath. "I do not want him to stop enjoying life or waiting around for my eventual death. If God wants to take my soul now, we should not interfere."

Tricia nodded sadly. Most patients with ALS were more afraid of being stuck within their minds than actual death. She understood, but she could not imagine what life would be like without Rebecca's gentle soul. "I will tell him," she said.

Leaving the room, Tricia traversed the hallways of the mansion. John had built his fortune by buying and selling real estate properties. His initial money had arrived through an early investment in the dot com boom before the bubble burst. After seeing the dangers of the stock market, he had started to just buy and rent out properties. Even with the recent recession, he still made a profit. Instead of selling his properties or developing, he had continued to rent them out. In a decade or two, he had talked of selling and retiring. His plans had arrived before his wife had been diagnosed with ALS. Unwilling to speak of his life after her future death, Tricia had not asked about any change in his future plans.

Knocking on the door, she heard a sound in the room and assumed that he was telling her to come in. She entered the office and John motioned for her to sit down. His tousled brown hair fell softly across his face and his icy blue eyes were focused intently on paperwork in front of him. Between running an empire and worrying about his wife, he seldom took time any more for his personal appearance. His face was growing a rugged stubble and looked like it had not seen a razor for a while. Dashing and muscular, his good looks had an almost otherworldly level of gorgeousness. John was known among business associates for his confidence and aggressive tactics. He played fair, but he managed his company with the best of his abilities.

If you like this sample, look for **<u>Love Anew - Lonely Billionaire Romance Series, Book 1 by Shyla Starr</u>**.

From the Author

If you enjoyed any of my books then please share the love and promote my books in Amazon.

If you write me a review and send me an email I will send you a free book, or many.
(Just know that these emails are filtered by my publisher.)

Good news is always welcome.

One Last Thing, For Kindle Readers...

When you turn the page, Kindle will give you the opportunity to rate this book and share your thoughts on Facebook and Twitter. If you enjoyed my writings, would you please take a few seconds to let your friends know about it? Because... when they enjoy they will be grateful to you and so will I.

Thank You!

Rocky Austin Quinn
rocky_austin_quinn@awesomeauthors.org